THE

NOT-MUCH
Sleepover Starring
GINGER
GREEN

The Not-Much Sleepover Starring Ginger Green
published in 2018 by
Hardie Grant Egmont
Ground Floor, Building 1, 658 Church Street
Richmond, Victoria 3121, Australia
www.hardiegrantegmont.com

 A catalogue record for this
book is available from the
National Library of Australia

Text copyright © 2018 Kim Kane
Illustrations copyright © 2018 Jon Davis
Series design copyright © 2018 Hardie Grant Egmont

Design by Stephanie Spartels
Internals typesetting by Kristy Lund-White

Printed in Australia by McPherson's Printing Group,
Maryborough, Victoria.

13 5 7 9 10 8 6 4 2

THE

NOT-MUCH
Sleepover Starring

GINGER
GREEN

BY KIM KANE
& JON DAVIS

hardie grant EGMONT

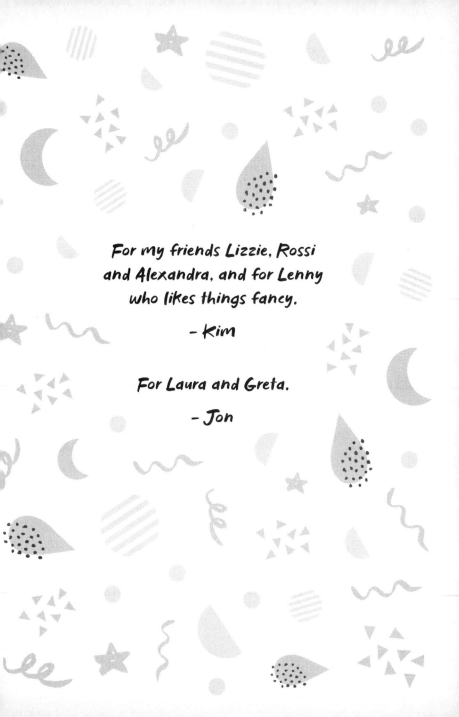

For my friends Lizzie, Rossi and Alexandra, and for Lenny who likes things fancy.

– Kim

For Laura and Greta.

– Jon

CHAPTER 1

'My name is **GINGER!** Ginger Green.'

I am eight years old.

When I was in grade two, I was **really** into play dates. Now I am in grade three, I am still into play dates but I am also into **bigger** kid things.

I am allowed to sleep on the top bunk at Grandma's.

so high!

I do not have to wear a skivvy with my school uniform in winter.

I have tried bubblegum, and ...

pop

2

I am allowed
to go on my

FIRST
EVER
SLEEPOVER!

I have **two** sisters, but so far
I am the **only one**
to go on a sleepover.

Violet is my
BIG sister.

We are both allowed to
sleep on the top bunk
and chew bubblegum, but
Violet does not
go on sleepovers
because she has no
friends, just books.

While books are
great, they do
not ask you on
sleepovers.

My LITTLE sister is Penny and she doesn't go on sleepovers either because she's

always nude.
Seriously.

Well, *mainly* nude.

Mum took her to kinder once in her undies and Penny was
not even a
SCRAP
embarrassed.
Not one scrap.
She just walked to the car like it was completely normal to wear a backpack with undies in the middle of winter.

rude!

5

Violet says Penny has
NO SHAME.

Penny says they have a **nude-food** policy at school, and if they have a **nude-food** policy

then there is nothing wrong with a **nude-kid** policy.

They also have a

NUT-FREE

policy and Penny

is **NUTS**, so quite

frankly she is going to

have to be careful.

But that's enough about my sisters, because

today is a very

SPECIAL DAY.

yay!

It is far too special to waste it talking about my sister who has **NO CLOTHES** and my sister who has **NO FRIENDS**.

Today is a very special day because I am going on a sleepover at my friend **Lottie's.**

Lottie is actually my very best friend this year.

Lottie is in my class at school and Lottie likes **EVERYTHING** that I like. Lottie likes cooking,

fun!

Lottie likes dancing,

Lottie likes **MixMatch** dolls ➤

... and gymnastics.

Lottie even likes rock climbing and pranks.

I am sure Lottie and I will both like sleepovers.

In fact, I am sure we will **LOVE** them.

For our sleepover, I have packed my **pyjamas**.
I have packed a **toothbrush** in a
special spotty sponge bag.
I have packed a **puffer vest**

in case it gets cold.
I have even packed

a *beanie*.

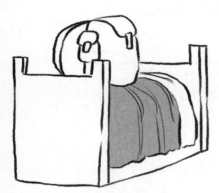

But I have not packed these things
because Lottie's house is cold.
Lottie's house is actually
very cosy.

I have packed these things because not

only am I going to have a sleepover at Lottie's,

I am going to sleep in a **TENT**.

We are going to
CAMP in Lottie's
back garden.

I thought I knew every single thing that Lottie likes
until she invited me to her house for a sleepover.
What I didn't know is that
Lottie **LOVES** camping.

Lottie just **LOVES** camping any way it comes.

Even in the **back** garden.
Probably in the **front** garden.
Probably even
in a **DISPLAY**
tent at the
camping
store.

My mum says there are two types of people in this world. There are people who camp and people who **don't**.

My mum is **NOT** a camper.

She says that when she has a holiday she does not want to make beds and cook. And if she has to do those things, she'd rather do them at home where she does not have to put up the walls as well.

so relaxing!

But Lottie
LOVES
CAMPING,

so I bet
I will love
camping
too.

How can I not?

CHAPTER 2

Mum drops me off at Lottie's house late in the afternoon. Lottie's mum is outside, painting the fence.

My mum waves goodbye.

'See you tomorrow morning!' she calls through the car window, and drives off.

'Well hello, Ginger Green!' says Lottie's mum. Lottie's mum is wearing overalls and she has a **shower cap** on her head. She pulls another shower cap from her pocket and hands it to me.

'Better put this on.'

'Oh,' I say.

I am puzzled.

I have never worn a shower cap before at a play date. I am not mad for shower caps. They are a bit itchy. But maybe shower caps are the way Lottie's family does sleepovers?

Maybe they are mad for shower caps like we are mad for pyjamas and slippers. I take the shower cap. 'Am I having a shower?' I ask.

'No,' says Lottie's mum. 'But you'll need to finish painting the fence before you go inside.'

I put down my backpack and pillow.

I had not expected that.

The WHOLE fence? I think.

The fence is **TALL**.
The fence is **LOOOOOONG**.

I pull on the shower cap. It itches.

huh?

'Is Lottie here?' I ask.

'No! Lottie's at your house,' says Lottie's mum. 'Didn't your mum tell you? Lottie has gone to your house to have a break. You have come to Lottie's house to **paint the fence**.'

She hands me a paintbrush.

I AM A BIT SHOCKED.

I am wearing a
SHOWER CAP
and I am painting
a fence.

'Why on earth did
Lottie go to
my house?'
I ask politely,
although
I am not
feeling that polite
at all.

Lottie's mum gives me a wink.
She laughs a really BIG belly laugh.

'PRANKED YOU!

LOTTIE'S INSIDE. LEAVE THE PAINTING TO ME AND GO AND HAVE FUN!'

I smile.
I smile
and laugh.

I forgot Lottie's mum **loves pranks.** I am not used to pranks at home. I am especially not used to *parents* pulling pranks.

LOL!

'Good one!' I say.

I pick up my backpack and pillow and go inside.

Lottie is in the kitchen, taking

biscuits from a jar.

'Ginger! Hi!'

Lottie looks very excited

to see me.

'Hi, Lottie!' I say.

'I forgot your mum pulls pranks!

she just got me
BIG time.'

'My mum is mad for camping and even madder for

pranks!' says Lottie. Lottie smiles her big friendly

smile. Then she takes me to the back door and points.

'Look!'

There, at the very back of the garden, is a silver tent. It is glinting like a SPACESHIP on the grass. There are some camp chairs folded against it.

'A TENT!'

I say.

'A first sleepover is **always** special. Camping at home is **very** special.'

Lottie and I **RUN** down to the tent.

We unzip the door.

'Careful of the mozzies,' says Lottie.

We step inside and
Lottie zips the door
back up quickly.
The light inside the
tent glows warmly.

The tent does smell
like old socks and mud,
but it is so **fun** and
so **exciting** I don't care.

25

I put my backpack and pillow inside the tent, and then Lottie and I run back to her house.

We grab two sleeping bags,

two camp mattresses

fun!

and a pillow for Lottie.

We grab a big torch.

Lottie's family camps
so much that they
have all the right gear.

Lottie and I lug all the right gear to the tent.

My family **does not** have camping gear.
Not even a torch.
My family has books and
MixMatch dolls.

Books and **MixMatch** dolls are great but they

are not much help when it comes to camping.

You just cannot sleep in a book or under

a **MixMatch** doll when it rains.

We roll out our mattresses. The mattresses are quite **FLAT** and as **THICK** as pancakes. They curl up at the ends. We spread out our sleeping bags so they match and we put down our pillows.

THIS MAY BE THE

MOST
EXCITING
NIGHT OF MY
LIFE.

Lottie goes inside and comes back with two bottles of water, two apples and four chocolate biscuits.

'This is our midnight feast,'

she says.

I smile. I have never had a sleepover. I have never been camping. I have never even had a midnight feast. A midnight feast sounds like great fun.

It is getting dark.
Midnight feels closer in winter.

Lottie balances the chocolate biscuits on the apples at the back of the tent. I line up the water bottles.

I am so excited that I squeal.
Lottie squeals too.
The tent looks so
cosy with all
our gear in it.
It looks so
delicious
with our
midnight
feast.

Fence-painting pranks and
shower caps seem a
long way away.
I am very excited

to be camping and very excited

to be on a **camping sleepover** at Lottie's.

I CANNOT WAIT FOR MIDNIGHT!

CHAPTER 3

While I was daydreaming about midnight feasts,

Lottie was daydreaming about ...

'**Dinner!**' says Lottie.

'We need to make dinner.

But first we

need a

FIRE.'

Lottie goes to the garage and drags out a big metal tub. It has holes in it.

It does not look like wood. It does not look like fire.

'What is it?' I ask.

'The inside of a washing machine,' says Lottie.

'A real one?' I ask.

'A real one!' says Lottie.

Well, that is unexpected.

'Are we going to do the washing?' I ask.

what?

Suddenly camping is not so great.

I am mad for play dates and sleepovers, but I actually am **NOT** mad for washing. It does not matter how you dress it up, washing is a chore. And chores are something you **HAVE** to do but not something you **WANT** to do.

ESPECIALLY ON A SLEEPOVER.

'We're not washing. Just watch,' says Lottie.

Lottie sets the washing machine tub on a pile of

BRICKS.

Lottie fills the washing machine tub with wood and chunks of coal. Lottie's mum comes out and helps light a real fire inside the real washing machine.

The fire burns high and bright.

It lets off lots of smoke.

We stoke the fire with a poker. Lottie's mum goes back to the kitchen and returns with a tray of sausages.

I turn around
to grab a
sausage and

SCREAM.

Lottie's mum's hand is covered in red.

Lottie's mum is holding the tray of sausages with a

BLOODY HAND!

'Are you OK? Quick, call an ambulance!'

I say.

Lottie's mum's hand looks very hurt. It does not look like it should be holding a tray of sausages.

But Lottie isn't worried. Lottie just rolls her eyes.

'MU-UM!'

Lottie's mum laughs.
'Pranked you!
It's a fake hand. Silly, isn't it?'

Lottie's mum pulls the fake hand from her sleeve and waves it. I laugh too. The fake hand has **THICK FAKE VEINS**. It has **THICK FAKE BLOOD**.

Now that it is waving at me, it looks very fake indeed.

'I saw it at the supermarket and I just couldn't resist,' says Lottie's mum.

'They had a fake hand at the supermarket?' I ask.

'Yes,' says Lottie's mum. '**In the HORROR aisle.**' She winks.

I laugh. 'They just have a cereal aisle at our supermarket,' I say. 'And fruit and veg.'

Lottie's mum tucks the fake hand in the pocket of her jeans. **It looks like it is waving at us.**

Lottie reaches out and shakes it by the fingertips. 'How do you do! I am Lottie.'

Lottie's mum smiles.

'Well Lottie, I thought you could cook your own sausages for dinner,' she says.

'**Is that a prank too?**' I ask.

I've never cooked dinner before. At home, I just make smoothies and salad dressing.

'No,' says Lottie. 'We **always** cook our own dinner when we are camping. **It's a treat!**'

Cooking sausages feels very **grown-up.**

That's the sort of thing you can do when you are in **grade three**. Actually, I don't think Violet has **EVER** cooked her own dinner and Violet is in grade five and reads books that are 300 pages long. If Violet ever goes camping she probably won't be able to cook her own dinner.

She might be forced to **EAT** her books.

At least they are 300 pages long. That should fill her up.

Cooking starts out fun. Lottie's mum goes back inside and we put the sausages on long forks and hold them over the coals.

They
SPIT AND SPAT
and go dark brown.

yum!

Lottie goes and gets a bowl of wet potatoes and a salt shaker. Lottie rubs salt into the jacket of each potato so it is evenly spread. **Lottie is very clever like that.**

I watch while Lottie wraps the potatoes in foil and throws them onto the coals. I take a small potato from the bowl. I wrap my own potato in foil and toss it onto the coals too.

≥ **THE FOIL GLOWS RED.** ≤

I swing my legs under my camp seat while I
wait for the potatoes to cook. The night
is getting cold, so Lottie collects our
vests and beanies from the tent.

We finish
toasting the
sausages.

We pile them on
our plates.

'That looks perfect,'
says Lottie. She pours sauce onto
her sausage. She pours on
so much sauce that her
sausage looks **BLOODIER**
than her mum's fake hand.

I take a bite of my sausage.

IT IS **RAW** IN THE MIDDLE AND **BLACK** ON THE OUTSIDE.

yuck!

The meat squeezes out like toothpaste
onto the paper plate.

Lottie uses tongs to take the potatoes out of the fire. She drops them on the ground.

I pick mine up from the grass.

The foil **burns** my fingers but the spud smells delicious. I take a bite. It is very hot. It is **black** on the outside and ...

RAW in the middle.

'I better not go on a cooking show,' says Lottie.

'Maybe not yet,' I grin.

Lottie looks around. 'Our dinner is burnt on the outside and raw on the inside. I'm not hungry anyway. We can't have dinner, but we can have some billy tea.'

'It's hard to burn tea,' I say.

It might be hard to burn tea but it turns out I do not like tea.

Burnt or not burnt. I do not like tea with milk. I do not like tea with sugar. Even with milk and sugar, tea still tastes like tea.

urgh!

Dinner has **not** been great and **I AM HUNGRY**, but I don't want to say so because it might make my friend feel bad. Lottie is not a very good camping cook, **but she did try.** At least we have a midnight feast for later.

We sit by the fire as it gets dark. We talk about **MixMatch** dolls and the class captain and who we might share a room with during school camp. We both put each other down as our number-one choice. We talk about Lottie's tonsils and my crazy smarty-pants birthday cake. We put more wood on the flames. Lottie starts to tell stories.

LOTTIE STARTS TO TELL
⇒ SCARY STORIES ⇐
ABOUT HEADLESS ZOMBIES.

The garden gets darker and colder. I snuggle closer
to the fire. The front of my body gets very **hot**.
But the back of my body is very **cold**. I am like a
piece of toast in a broken toaster – burnt on one
side but still just bread on the other. I pull down
my beanie.

I look back towards the house. I can see inside Lottie's kitchen. I can see Lottie's mum and dad at the table eating spaghetti. I can just spy the playroom behind them.

The house looks bright and warm.

I was so excited about this camping sleepover. Now I just want to have a **proper dinner** inside Lottie's house with carpet and heating and Lottie's mum's pranks. I want to be a piece of toast cooked on **BOTH SIDES**.

Lottie yawns. 'Shall we go **INSIDE** the tent, where it is **COSY**?'

I look at my watch. 'It is only six-thirty!'

'There is not much to do without daylight,' says Lottie.

I want to point out to Lottie that there is in fact a lot to do without daylight. There is actually an entire house behind us that has **light switches** and heating and heaps of toys and a dinner that is cooked all the way through and does not **OOZE** like toothpaste.

But I say nothing. Lottie loves camping and I do not want to make her feel bad. I do not want her to feel bad even though she wants to go to bed earlier than Penny does. A lot earlier.

'Let's hit the sack,' says Lottie.

'Or the sleeping bag,' I say.

At least it will be warmer in the sleeping bag, I think.

It certainly can't be any colder.

Lottie smiles. We leave the fire and walk over

to the tent. When we get to the tent, it is clear

SOMETHING IS WRONG.

Lottie shines her torch at the tent.

The tent door is **OPEN**. And there are

chocolate biscuit crumbs everywhere.

CHAPTER 4

The chocolate biscuit crumbs are sprinkled **all over the floor.** The tent door flaps in the wind.

'I must have left it open when I came back to get our beanies,' says Lottie. **'Oops! Sorry!** The good news is that it's **too cold for mozzies now.'**

TOO COLD FOR MOZZIES?

It is too cold for life! In fact, if I look hard enough I might see mozzies **frozen solid in iceblocks** on the ground.

We go into the tent and look around.

Lottie shines the torch.

The water bottles are fine but one apple has **BITE MARKS** all over it. The other apple is **gone**. And there is **nothing left** of the chocolate biscuits but chocolate biscuit **crumbs**.

'What happened? Is it another prank?'

I ask, full of hope.

Lottie shakes her head. 'I don't think so.' She picks
up the apple and looks at the TEETH MARKS.
'I think something got into the tent.
That will teach me not
to zip it up.'

'A ZOMBIE?' I ask.

Lottie laughs.
'Whatever it was, it has **SHARP TEETH**
and it likes apples and chocolate biscuits
for dinner.'

eek!

So do I,
I think.
The rat
certainly
didn't come and
steal the raw
sausages or
the billy tea.

We sweep out the tent.

The tent does not feel as exciting as it felt
in the afternoon. The tent feels like
it might have fleas.

IT FEELS DIRTY.

It also feels cold.

We get changed into our PJs. I am freezing.
I put my vest and beanie back on. We both leave
our socks on.

'Is camping always this cold?' I ask.

'Always,' says Lottie. 'Sometimes, it's even colder.

Once it even **SNOWED**.'

In the tent?
I wonder.

Lottie does not sound unhappy that it is cold. In fact, Lottie sounds quite happy. Lottie does not seem to worry that we ate **RAW SAUSAGES FOR DINNER**. Or actually didn't eat at all. Lottie doesn't seem to worry that the tent already feels damp. Lottie doesn't even seem worried that our midnight feast has just disappeared and that *whatever* took it **might just come back**.

'I LOVE camping,' says Lottie, climbing into her sleeping bag.

She shines the torch up at the wall of the tent. **'I love everything about it.'**

I slip into my sleeping bag. My tummy is rumbling. It is rumbling **SO LOUDLY** I can hear it through the sleeping bag. It is rumbling so loudly that Lottie says, 'What's that?'

I say nothing. I do not want Lottie to know that her friend has a tummy that sounds like a zombie. A hungry headless zombie.

why?

I lie back. I want to look at my toes in a sleeping bag. I tip my legs up. I feel a bit like a caterpillar. I am just like the **Very Hungry Caterpillar** only I am cold as well.

Lottie tips her legs up too.

We wriggle like caterpillars together.

Lottie shines the torch. She makes shadow creatures on the side of the tent. Lottie is **BRILLIANT** at shadow creatures.

She makes a duck, →

a spider & and a ...

BOX.

"

"

'A box!' I laugh.

'You're meant to make creatures, not things!'

'I do **Shadow Randoms** when I am camping,' says Lottie. 'Shadow Randoms are much more interesting!'

'Like this?' ⟶

I pinch my fingers and make an **O**.

'What is it?' asks Lottie.

'The left eye of a pair of goggles.

There's your Shadow Random.'

I giggle too.

Soon Lottie **yawns**. 'I am always tired camping,' she says sleepily. 'Bed early and up early. Night, Ginger. Sorry about our midnight feast.' She turns over and turns off the torch.

'Night, Lottie.'

grumble!

I lie in bed. After two minutes, Lottie starts to breathe quietly.

She is
ASLEEP!

what?

already?

HOW does Lottie do that?

How can Lottie sleep at a time like **THIS?**

I CANNOT SLEEP.

I lie awake. My mattress is lumpy.

ouch!

A pancake is the perfect thickness for breakfast but it is not the perfect thickness for a mattress. I feel like the **Princess and the Pea**. I can feel every tiny bump from the ground in my back.

I TURN.
AND I
TURN.

I am so **hungry**

it is hard to sleep.

I am so **uncomfortable**

it is hard to sleep.

And then there is a sound.

I HEAR CRUNCHING.

what's that?

I hear the crunching of a
BONE-CRUSHING ZOMBIE.

I hear the crunching of a

bone-crushing zombie

getting closer.

This time it is **NOT** my tummy.

Even my tummy is in shock.

CRUNCH.

CRUNCH.

I see a bone-crushing zombie's shadow outside. I see the shadow on the wall of the tent. It is a **MASSIVE** Shadow Random. It is two metres high with an enormous thick head. It has no face. It has no nose. It has no mouth. It is not the midnight-feast-stealing rat.

It is just **TOO BIG.**

CRUNCH.
CRUNCH.

LOTTIE SLEEPS ON.

The great big zombie bends down.

The zip creaks.

I pull my sleeping

bag up to my eyes. I stare.

I don't breathe.

LOTTIE
SLEEPS
ON.

I SCREAM.

The zip **creaks** as it is pulled open. A huge hand with three thick fingers comes around the corner.

The door opens.

The side of the tent **shakes**.

AND **THEN** ...

CHAPTER 5

A GIANT YELLOW HEAD

bobs into the tent.

There is a laugh.

I see a banana.
A giant banana
is coming into the
tent laughing with
a big belly laugh.
The giant banana
waves a torch.

'No,' I whisper. 'Don't eat me.'

'Ginger, it's okay,' says the banana.

The giant banana knows my name! I scream again.
The giant banana lifts its three fingers and rips off
its head.

I scream again.

'AHHHHHHHHHHHHHHHHHHHHHHHH!'

'Ginger, it's just me!'

Under the giant banana head is **Lottie's mum.** Lottie's mum is in the tent in the middle of the night. Lottie's mum is in the tent in the middle of the night **wearing a giant banana costume.**

⇒ **WITHOUT A HEAD.** ⇐

'Ginger, I am so sorry, I thought this was a hoot. I brought it home from work. **We love pranks.** I thought you girls would both think it was funny. I would **NEVER** have done it if I thought it would scare you.'

'Oh,' I say in a little voice.

Lottie's mum is mad.
In fact, **LOTTIE'S MUM IS BANANAS.**

Lottie's mum gives me a hug. Being hugged by a giant banana actually feels quite nice. She shines her torch around the tent. Lottie is still asleep. 'Is everything all right now?'

I blink.

EVERYTHING IS NOT ALL RIGHT.

I AM
SCARED.

I was scared before Lottie's
mum turned up in a giant
banana costume.
I AM SCARED
camping outside.
I AM TIRED and I AM SORE.
I AM HUNGRY.

I am staying with a friend whose mum thinks it is
funny to scare kids in a tent. I am staying with a
friend whose mum thinks it is funny to scare kids
in a giant banana costume.

IT IS **NOT** ALL RIGHT TO SCARE KIDS IN A TENT WITH A GIANT BANANA COSTUME.

I do not like camping and I do not like pranks.

And suddenly it is very clear to me.

I don't want to be at Lottie's anymore.

Suddenly I want **MY BED** and **MY BEDROOM** with Violet reading under her reading light. I don't want strange smells and strange sounds and maybe bone-crushing-zombies. I definitely don't want giant bananas.

84

Camping **seemed** exciting when Lottie spoke about it at school, but it is not feeling exciting now. **I want to go home.**

Lottie *finally* wakes up. 'Hi Mum,' she says, and rubs her eyes. 'What are you wearing?'

'A giant banana costume.'

Lottie starts to laugh. **'That is hilarious.'**

'It gave Ginger a bit of a fright,' says Lottie's mum. 'It's very cold – even in this giant banana costume. And it feels like it is about to rain. It might be best to come inside.'

I wait for Lottie to say **NO**.

I wait for Lottie to say she **LOVES** camping and raw sausages and being too hot by the fire and too cold everywhere else. I wait for Lottie to say she loves frights and pranks and billy tea and giant banana costumes. I wait for Lottie to say all these things.

Instead, she says, 'Good idea. Let's camp inside.'

And then I remember **WHY** Lottie is my **BEST FRIEND**.

CHAPTER 6

We grab our pillows.
We grab our
sleeping bags.

And we RUN.

We run all the way across the back garden
in our socks. We run in the drizzling rain.

We get inside. We are a
BIT DIRTY and a
BIT WET
and

VERY
COLD.

We shiver.

'Let's put you in the shower,' says Lottie's mum.
'That will warm you up.'

Lottie's mum helps us turn on the shower.
She hands me a thick towel. She does not
even mention shower caps.

When we get out of the shower, Lottie's mum has taken the cushions off the couch and put them under the dining room table.

I go to sit on the couch. The couch looks hard without cushions. 'Is this another prank?' I ask.

'I am getting the hang of pranks!'

'No!' says Lottie. 'Just wait. It's camping inside!'

Lottie grabs some blue blankets and hangs them over the table. We each drag our sleeping bag into the blue-blanket tent. Lottie has a torch. We are wearing clean pyjamas.

Lottie's mum brings us hot milk with cinnamon.

cosy!

We finish the milk but we are **still hungry.**

'What about pancakes?' asks Lottie. 'We can make our own dinner when we're camping inside too.'

Lottie and I mix eggs and flour and milk and vanilla.

We put butter in the pan and watch as it
⇒ **sizzles.** ⇐

We make six round pancakes and then I make a long thin one.

'That's a funny shape!' says Lottie. 'Is it a giant banana?'

I laugh. 'It's a PANCAKE RANDOM.'

When the pancakes are ready we pour a little **honey** on them.

We take the honey pancakes back to our tent. We lie under the blue-blanket tent on the couch cushions. Lottie hands me a fork.

yum!

I take a bite. The pancakes are cooked **all the way through.** 'Delicious,' I say.

'Pancakes are the PERFECT dinner,' says Lottie.

I roll over on the couch cushions.

'Pancakes are certainly much better to eat than to sleep on,' I say.

comfy!

I smile. I am no longer scared. I am no longer cold and I am no longer hungry. In fact, I am very, very comfy.

After we have done our teeth, we lie in the blanket tent and read. Lottie's mum tiptoes in to give us a **kiss**. 'Well, Ginger Green, I am very sorry that I frightened you,' she says.

'That's okay,' I say. 'I guess it actually was funny. My mum just doesn't do things like that.'

'You mum doesn't dress up in a giant banana costume?' says Lottie's mum. 'What on earth does she do with her time?'

I LAUGH.

'What did you think of your first camping experience?' Lottie's mum asks.

I THINK.

I do not want to hurt Lottie's feelings but **I do want to tell the truth.**

'I love the sleepover part and the shadow randoms and reading in this blue-blanket tent, but

I am not mad on camping. Not outdoors anyway.'

Lottie's mum laughs again.

'I love camping **anywhere**,'

says Lottie. 'By the beach, in the snow, in

the back garden **and** under the dining room table.'

'That's because there are two types of people in life,

Lottie,' I tell her. '**People who camp.**

And people who don't. Lottie, you

are a kid who does. I am a kid who does not. I still

like sleepovers, though, and I LOVE honey pancakes.

Especially pancake randoms. Oh, and I do like pranks.

Just **NOT** in the middle of the night.'

* ★ ✱ ★ ★ ★ *

THE NEXT MORNING,

Lottie and I eat **cornflakes** at the kitchen bench and put all the cushions back on the couch. We fold the blankets and tie my dirty clothes up in a plastic bag.

When Mum arrives, I run out and give her a hug.
She hugs me back. She is wearing jeans and her
favourite jumper.

She does **NOT** have
a fake bloody hand.

She is **NOT** wearing
a shower cap.

I hug
her
harder.

'How was your sleepover?' she says.

'**FUN,**' I say. 'But **promise me** you won't **ever** come and visit in the middle of the night in a giant banana costume.'

Lottie laughs.

Mum looks puzzled. 'That, Ginger Green, is one promise that will not be hard to keep.'

I laugh too. Then I hand Mum the plastic bag of pyjamas.

'If you're **BIG** enough for camping, you're **BIG** enough for washing,' says Mum.

'I'll show you how to work the washing machine when we get home.'

'Can I light a fire in it?' I ask. 'You light a fire in a washing machine when you camp.'

Mum looks shocked.

'YOU LIT A FIRE?'

I nod. 'And we cooked our own dinner on it.'

Mum laughs.

'Cooking your own dinner?! My Ginger Green is all **GROWN-UP**.'

'Not a very good dinner,' I say. 'A bit of a **BURNT** dinner.'

'And a bit of a raw dinner,' adds Lottie.

'I think I'll stick to making smoothies and salad dressing for now. **And honey pancakes!'**

I turn around to Lottie.

'Lottie, next time we can have a sleepover at **my house.** I can make you a smoothie and we can sleep under our dining room table.'

'**That does sound fun,**' grins Lottie.

I pick up my
backpack and pillow.
It's time to go home.

'**Bye Lottie!**'

I say.

I am **Ginger Green**
and I am just a bit bigger now.

fun!

I am BIG
enough

to go on a

sleepover

and even big enough

to go **camping**.

I am big enough to **cook my own**
pancakes.

It turns out different people's families do different things.

Some families camp,

Some families don't.

Some mums wear jeans and find films funny.

Other mums wear giant banana costumes and find those funny.

I am **NOT** mad for camping or middle-of-the-night pranking, but I am mad for sleepovers. **I cannot wait** to have a sleepover again soon!

THE END

HOW TO PLAN YOUR OWN Not-Much Sleepover

GINGER'S
Perfect
INDOORS TABLE
CAMPING

Even though I am <u>not mad</u> for outdoors camping,

Lottie has really got me into indoors camping. To make the perfect inside tent, find a big, stable table. A kitchen table or dining room table is usually perfect.

Ping-pong tables can also work really well ↘

... **and even billiard tables work** (if you happen to live in castle that has one).

↓

Put couch cushions or mattresses under the table.

Sometimes I use the mattress from our fold-out bed. Sometimes I use the cushions from the couch even if Violet is reading on them.

Violet is not mad on that. ➔

hey!

Put a sheet over your cushions (so crumbs from your midnight feast don't stain them).

I learnt this the hard way. If you flip up our couch you can still see the stains from a melted Chocolate Royal under the cushion. Who knew Chocolate Royals could do that much damage?!

Plan a spot for a special midnight feast.

I put the snacks and water bottles in a plastic container and put it where it's hard to kick over. (Dad makes me get up and clean my teeth after a midnight feast, which is annoying, but choc–chip biscuits taste **so much better** in the middle of the night that it's worth it.)

Bring a torch, pillows and doonas or blankets in under the table.

Hang blankets or sheets around the edge of the table.

Secure them by putting heavy books on top. Just make sure the books are in towards the middle of the table so they don't slip down on top of you!

To join the blankets at the sides, I peg them with pegs from the clothesline but I always leave one blanket unpegged for a door. Sometimes I even peg that when I am inside with Lottie and need to keep No-Pants Penny **OUT**.

keep out!

If you turn on the torch inside the tent you can make shadow randoms on the wall with your hands.

TRY:

A donut with a bite out of it.

A left goggle.

A bald head.

A bald cupcake.

If you don't have a table you can always make

GINGER'S DOONA COCOON FOR ONE.

Use pegs to clip one end of your doona to the top of a chair. Then fold the other end of the doona over to make a hammock, and clip that end to the chair as well. Now you can crawl into the perfect doona cocoon for one. I usually read in mine and sometimes I even draw.

snuggly!

LOTTIE + GINGER'S
Pancake Randoms

STEP 1 Mix together 2 eggs, 1 cup of milk and 1 cup of flour.

Mum makes me use half buckwheat flour and half self-raising flour if she is going through a healthy phase. Otherwise I just use self-raising. I use an electric mixer to get out all the lumps.

STEP 2 Get a grown-up to turn on the stove and heat the frying pan.

STEP 3 Put butter in the hot frying pan and dodge the spits!

STEP 4 Pour in the mixture any way you want.

I usually use about 3 tablespoons per pancake. Sometimes I criss-cross the mixture over the pan to make #hashtag pancakes, sometimes I do big wonky hats or even a giant banana. Just don't go too big or fancy or they break when you flip them.

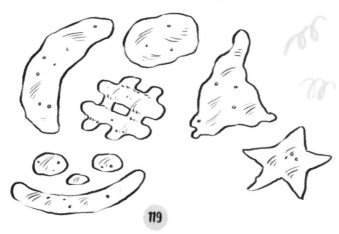

STEP 5 I cover my Pancake Randoms in butter and honey or butter, cinnamon and sugar but you could even go really random with your toppings. Popping candy and chocolate sauce, anyone? Peanut butter and marshmallow? Soy sauce and ice-cream?

ULTIMATE CHALLENGE: Try to make your pancakes shaped like your Shadow Randoms.

About the author and illustrator

KIM KANE is an award-winning Australian author who writes for children and teens. Her books include the CBCA short-listed picture book *Family Forest*, and her time-slip children's novel *When the Lyrebird Calls*. **Ginger Green** is the second series starring this funny and feisty fox. Ginger first appeared in *Ginger Green, Play Date Queen*, a beloved first-reader series.

Pirates, old elephants, witches in bloomers, bears on bikes, ugly cats, sweet kids - **JON DAVIS** does it all! Based in the Lake District, England, Jon Davis has illustrated more than 60 kids' books for publishers across the globe, including *Ginger Green, Play Date Queen!*

Acknowledgements

I would like to thank the HGE team including Penny, Luna and Marisa, who could not be more tapped into our readership if they were eight themselves, and Hilary, with whom it all began. To Jon, Steph and Kristy for turning the words into illustrations and beautiful designs. I would like to thank my Australian agent Pippa, who fights contracts while raising a future readership. I would like to thank Jane who is a wonderful, fun mum and who wore the banana suit as a PRANK for her kids – and of course Ben, Lachlan, Ellie (and Will!) who survived the banana suit and lived to tell the tale. Finally, I would like to acknowledge my children and their friends, whose quips and antics I shall shamelessly plunder for as long as they will let me. With love and thanks. – *Kim*

Thanks to Kim and the Hardie Grant Egmont chaps for giving me the chance to illustrate such fab books. – *Jon*

Have you
read
EVERY

GINGER
GREEN

book?

THE NOT-MUCH Sleepover Starring GINGER GREEN

BY KIM KANE & JON DAVIS

GINGER GREEN IS ABSOLUTELY MAD FOR Birthdays (mostly)

BY KIM KANE & JON DAVIS

Coming soon!

GINGER GREEN on the (UN)LUCKIEST Camp Ever!

BY KIM KANE & JON DAVIS

GINGER GREEN IS ABSOLUTELY MAD FOR Birthdays!

(mostly)

Ginger is turning **EIGHT** and she's having an **exceptionally royal PRINCESS PARTY**. There will be crowns, a **FANCY** castle cake AND EVEN → **SPARKLE SLIME**.

But what happens when **Crazy Maisy** and **No-Pants Penny** get out of control?

GINGER GREEN
on the
(UN)LUCKIEST Camp
Ever!

Ginger **KNOWS** that she is going to **LOVE** school camp – it's got **sing-a-longs, bunk beds** and → **RED JELLY** ← **GALORE!**

But what happens when she's put in **Cabin Four**, the **UNLUCKIEST** cabin of all?

GINGER GREEN on the (UN)LUCKIEST Camp Ever!

BY KIM KANE & JON DAVIS

DO YOU HAVE A YOUNGER SIBLING WHO **LOVES** LISTENING TO YOU READ GINGER GREEN?

Maybe they'd like to read:

Meet Maisy, Daya, Isla and more of Ginger's friends when they were younger, and **LOVED** having play dates!

Ginger is **BRIMMING** with excitement, **BURSTING** to dance and **BUSTING** to play with her friends!

Have you read every Ginger Green, Play Date Queen?